snore!

For Tom and Oliver
and Daniel the Artist
JL

This edition published in Picture Lions in Great Britain by HarperCollins Publishers Ltd 1999.
First published in hardback in Great Britain by HarperCollins Publishers Ltd 1998.

1 3 5 7 9 10 8 6 4 2

ISBN 0 00 664 639-5

Picture Lions is an imprint of the Children's Division, part of HarperCollins Publishers Ltd,
77–85 Fulham Palace Road, Hammersmith, London, W6 8JB.

Text © Michael Rosen 1998
Illustrations © Jonathan Langley 1998

A CIP catalogue record for this title is available from the British Library.

Printed and bound in Singapore by Imago.

snore!

Michael Rosen

illustrated by Jonathan Langley

PictureLions

An Imprint of HarperCollins*Publishers*

All was quiet on the farm.

Dog was asleep.   Cat was asleep.

Cow was asleep.

Sheep was asleep.

Pig was asleep,

and so were all the Piglets.

It was all so peaceful – till...

snore!

and Cat woke up.

Cow woke up.

Sheep woke up.

Pig woke up, and so did all the Piglets.

It was so loud no one could sleep,
not Cat, or Cow, or Sheep, or Pig,
nor all the Piglets.

snore!

How can we get Dog to stop snoring
so we can all get back to sleep?
said Cat.

I know, said Cow – and Cow
went up to Dog and went
ATTISSHOOO
right down his ear.

snore!

I know, said Sheep – and Sheep
went up to Dog and
went **BOO** right
down his ear.

snore!

I know, said Pig – and Pig went up to Dog and went **HEE HEE** right down his ear, and all the Piglets went **HEE HEE HEE HEE.**

snore!

I know, said Cat, why don't we
sing to him?

Maybe that'll stop him snoring and we can all go back to sleep.

So Cat went **PURRRR.**

snore!

And Cow went **MOOO.**

snore!

And Sheep went
BAAA.

snore!

And Pig went **OINK** and all the Piglets went **GRUNT GRUNT GRUNT GRUNT.**

snore!

Then as the sun rose over the trees,
Rooster woke up with a
**COCK-A-DOODLE-
DOOOOO,**

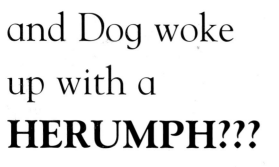

and Dog woke
up with a
HERUMPH???

And off he trotted down the
road after his good night's sleep.

But Cat and Cow and Sheep and
Pig and all the Piglets were so tired...
they fell asleep.

snore!

snore!